The Frog King

AN AFRICAN FOLKTALE

retold by Amanda StJohn • illustrated by Karen Perrins

The Child's World

Distributed by The Child's World®
1980 Lookout Drive • Mankato, MN 56003-1705
800-599-READ • www.childsworld.com

Acknowledgments
The Child's World®: Mary Berendes, Publishing Director
The Design Lab: Kathleen Petelinsek, Design
Red Line Editorial: Editorial direction

Library of Congress Cataloging-in-Publication Data
StJohn, Amanda, 1982–
  The frog king : an African folktale / by Amanda StJohn ; illustrated by
Karen Perrins.
       p. cm.
  Summary: In Kenya, Africa, an old frog named Mahday awakens the god
Mmumi to ask for a king who will help the frogs to get along better with
other creatures, but Mmumi does not like to be awakened and sends an
unpleasant answer to her request. Includes notes.
  ISBN 978-1-60973-137-3 (library reinforced : alk. paper)
  [1. Folklore–Kenya.] I. Perrins, Karen, ill. II. Title.
  PZ8.1.S8577Fro 2012
  398.2096762'045—dc23   2011010891

Printed in the United States of America in Mankato, Minnesota.
July 2011
PA02086

*ambo, jambo*. Hello, hello. Don't be shy. Gather close to me. I have a wonderful story, a wonderful story to tell, indeed.

In Kenya, Africa, at the dawn of time, there lived some frogs. These frogs needed a king who could teach them to be respectful of all the animals in the world. If only the frogs had learned this on their own, things would not have been so bad. . . .

From the first day of the world, frogs lived on Lake Nyanza. *Eeep, errrp. Eeep, errrp. . . . Grrrop. Grrrop. Grrrop.* All day and all night, the frogs played. They danced and swam. They ate and sang. Can you imagine all the fun those frogs had?

They croaked so loudly that a roaring lion could not be heard near the lake!

One night, all the animals of the world came to talk to the frogs.

"Frogs," said the antelope, "we cannot sleep with all this noise!"

"Frogs," said the fish, "you kick us with your feet and do not even say you're sorry!"

"I can't even hear myself *roar!*" the lioness roared.

Well, the frogs liked to have their fun. But they didn't mean to bother the other animals in the world. The frogs decided that something must be done. But, what?

"We need a king!" said Mahday, the oldest frog. Everyone agreed with her, but whom would they choose?

All the frogs began to talk at once.

"I'm the strongest!" said one frog.

"I'm the loudest!" said another.

And so it went until all the frogs were fighting to be the new king.

Mahday croaked into a hollow log. "Quiet! Quiiiiiiiiiet!" Her voice cracked like thunder across the lake and echoed across the whole world. The frogs gasped with surprise.

"No one here can be king of frogs,"
said Mahday. "We fight too much." The
frogs nodded in agreement. Mahday said,
"We must wake the god Mmumi and ask
him to give us a king."

The frogs gasped again. One frog
shrieked and dove under water to hide.

Mmumi was a cranky god—every one knew that. He liked to sleep—and he did not like to be awakened.

Seeing how afraid the frogs were, Mahday knew that she would have to wake Mmumi herself.

"*Jambo*, Mmumi." Mahday whispered the magic words to instantly wake the sleeping god.

"Huh? What?" Mmumi rubbed his sleepy eyes and yawned. "Who dares to wake Mmumi now? Does she want to be eaten?"

"I am not tasty," croaked Mahday in her old woman's voice. Then she told Mmumi the frogs' problem. "Give us a king to teach us respect, and I will let you sleep again."

"Fine, fine," said Mmumi.

Then Mahday spoke the magic words to put him back to sleep. "*Lala salama.* Sleep well."

The next day, Mahday and the frogs were in the lake playing, swimming, and making noise, noise, noise.

Splash! Something hit the water. It sank to the bottom of the lake and settled in some reeds.

The mysterious creature didn't move. He didn't come up to breathe. He didn't eat.

The voice of Mmumi came sweeping by on the wind. It said, "Here is your king. Respect him, and be happy."

For days, the frogs swam quietly about. They feared the king was tired, like Mmumi. They didn't want to wake him. They didn't want to step on him, either. And, if the king should wake up and want to speak, they wanted to hear him.

Then, one day, two young frogs became tired of being so quiet. They dove under water to see the frog king.

Boioioioing! One little frog sprang out in front of his king, making a silly face. Then, he hid again.

Boioioing! The other little frog sprang out in front of her king. She stuck out her tongue and sang, "Nah, nah. You can't get me!"

But the frog king didn't move.

Finally, the little frogs went over to the frog king and knocked on his head. "Huh?" The frog king was not a frog. He was not even a king. He was a plain, old rock!

Soon, no one respected the frog king. The frogs danced and played and made lots of noise all day and all night as they had before.

Immediately, Mahday went to Mmumi. "*Jambo*, Mmumi," she said, waking the grumpy god.

"We need a new king, Mmumi," she said. "One that will always be respected." Mmumi smiled a terrible smile, showing all his long teeth. "Fine, fine . . ." he said.

Mahday felt uneasy about Mmumi's toothy smile, but she put him back to sleep as promised. "*Lala salama*. Sleep well."

That night, the frogs were noisier than ever. They were celebrating their freedom from the old frog king.

Not one frog, not even Mahday, noticed the creeping shadow at the edge of the lake. No one saw the delicate ripples spreading toward them. No one saw the bright yellow eyes floating on the water like little lanterns.

Snap! Snap! Huge jaws came lunging out of the water. It was Mamba, the first crocodile in the world.

Mamba gobbled up some frogs. He thrashed about, whacking frogs with his large tail. All along, he flashed a large, toothy smile—just like the one Mmumi had shown Mahday.

Then, for no good reason, Mamba slipped away as quietly as a whisper.

The next day, the frogs did not make too much noise. They made some noise, and they ate some food, and they swam a little bit.

Sometimes, a young frog would croak a beautiful note. It would inspire the other frogs, and each would do the same. Then, everyone would be singing, all together. *Eeep, errp. Eeep, errp. Grrrop! Grrrop! Grrrop!*

All the frogs would sing their beautiful songs until someone heard any tiny noise—the swish of a fish's tail or the footsteps of a person. Then, everyone would lunge into the water and hide, perfectly still, like the first frog king. In this way, the frogs always respected their new king, Mamba.

AFRICA

FOLKTALES

The Frog King is a story from Kenya, Africa. It comes from an area near Lake Nyanza, also called Lake Victoria. We know this because, in 1973, a man named Humphrey Harman went to the lake and visited African tribal peoples living there. He loved to listen to the great storytellers, and he wrote down what he heard. Once, these stories were only shared by word of mouth. Now that they are written down, people all over the world can enjoy African folktales, such as *The Frog King.*

The common language spoken in Kenya is Swahili. Even though each African tribe has its own language, most people can also speak Swahili. The African words used in this version of *The Frog King* are also Swahili.

You've already learned *jambo*, which means "hello," and *lala salama*, which means "sleep well." But Mahday and Mamba are characters whose names come from Swahili words. Mahday, or more correctly *Madey*, means mother. Mahday always seems to know just what to do, and the other frogs listen to her when she speaks. In this way, she is like a mother to the other frogs. As for Mamba, his name means, "big fish."

Folktales not only tell a story, they share a lesson, too. One thing that *The Frog King* teaches us is to speak in a soft voice when playing in a space shared with lots of other people—remember the lion who wanted to hear herself roar? That's just one of the ways that the folktale teaches about showing respect to others.

ABOUT THE ILLUSTRATOR

Karen Perrins lives in central England with her partner and cats. She loves working in her garden studio using paints, pastels, watercolors and printmaking techniques—all while listening to loud music! Apart from illustrating, Karen's favorite pastimes are going on vacation and cooking. She also runs printmaking workshops in local art galleries.